TRIPLE TROUBLE

MICHAEL J. PELLOWSKI

cover art by Gabriel
inside illustration by Mel Crawford

To
T.G.O.G.

Published by Willowisp Press
801 94th Avenue North, St. Petersburg, Florida 33702

Copyright © 1995 by Willowisp Press,
a division of PAGES, Inc.
Original Edition © 1988 by Willowisp Press

Printed in the United States of America

2 4 6 8 10 9 7 5 3 1

ISBN 0-87406-724-1

One

"RANDI, make Teddy a sandwich, please," Mom called down from upstairs. "He's hungry."

Teddy is our three-year-old brother. And he's always hungry.

I lowered the book I was reading and glanced over at my twin sister, Randi. She was sprawled on the living room sofa. Her nose was buried in the sports section of the newspaper. Randi has two passions in life. One is sports. The other is any article of clothing that's bright red. At that very moment, she had on a bright red warm-up suit, red sneakers, and a red baseball cap.

I like things a little simpler than Randi does.

I like pink and purple. I like feminine dresses. I like reading romance novels that make me cry. And I hate to admit it, but I almost like doing homework. Admitting that isn't too bad when school is out for the summer. But I'd never say that during the school year. After all, hating homework—or at least pretending to—is kind of like a school tradition.

I looked at Randi and shook my head. I knew that she'd heard Mom call her and she still hadn't moved a muscle. If Mom had called me, I'd be up already. For two kids who are identical twins, we really aren't a lot alike. We sure look alike, especially since I traded in my glasses for contacts, but most of the time, we don't think or act alike.

"Randi? Randi!" Mom yelled again. "Did you hear what I said?"

"I'll get Teddy a sandwich, Mom," I shouted as I got up off my chair.

Randi lowered her paper. "I was just going to do it," she said.

"Sure you were," I said sarcastically. "You know, Randi, Mom and Dad are busy getting ready for our cousin Mandy's visit. The least you could do would be to make your little brother a sandwich."

"I've helped as much as you have," Randi replied. "Besides, there's nothing left to do. Mom and Dad have been fussing over this visit for weeks." Randi paused and then continued. "You know, I'm almost sick of hearing about our cute California cousin who's headed for stardom."

Just then Teddy came thundering down the steps from upstairs. Mom and Dad were up there putting an extra bed in our room for the famous Mandy. It was the final touch before Mandy arrived tomorrow.

"I helpin' Mom," Teddy said as he reached the bottom of the steps.

"I'll bet," I joked as I gently pinched Teddy's cheeks. He looks like a little angel. But he hardly ever acts like one. Where Teddy goes, trouble follows. In fact, "Trouble" is one of our favorite nicknames for Teddy.

"Come on, Teddy. I'll get you something to eat," I said as I moved toward the kitchen. Randi finally rolled off the couch and followed us.

I went to work on a peanut butter sandwich just the way Teddy likes it—with lots of strawberry jelly.

Randi finally decided to help, and turned to Teddy. "What do you want to drink, kiddo?"

"I want moze," Teddy said. "Moze" is Teddy's baby word for milk.

Randi opened the refrigerator, took out the milk, and slammed the door.

"Don't swamm da frigafrator," Teddy said in a scolding voice. He sounded just like Dad when Dad complains about the same thing.

"Listen, Peewee," Randi said as she poured his milk. "You can't tell me what to do. I'm your big sister. I tell you what to do. I'm your boss."

Teddy made a face at Randi. "You not da boss," he said. "Daddy da boss an' Mommy da boss. You not a boss." He grabbed his sandwich

7

and began to nibble on it.

I couldn't help but laugh. "I guess he told you," I teased Randi. Then I looked back at Teddy. I don't know how he did it, but Trouble had managed to drip big globs of strawberry jelly all over himself. "Teddy, watch what you're doing. Eat right!" I scolded.

"You not da boss either," Teddy said. "Ranee, Sanee not da boss." And then he picked up his glass of milk and stomped off to the living room.

I looked at Randi. She looked at me. We both burst out laughing at exactly the same time. Even though we are different in so many ways, we are always doing or thinking the same thing at the same time.

"Come on, Boss," Randi said. "Let's see if Mom and Dad need any help."

"Okay, Boss," I replied. "We'd better make sure everything is ready when our California cousin arrives tomorrow. We can't disappoint the star of a candy commercial, can we?"

"I wonder if she's changed a lot," Randi said as we climbed the stairs. "It's been a long time since we've seen her."

"Anything can happen to someone who spends years living in Hollywood," I said. "Mandy will be here tomorrow, and we'll know for sure."

Two

THE next day came before we knew it, and we were all headed to the airport to pick up Mandy.

"I can't wait to see Mandy," Mom said in a bubbly tone as Dad steered the car toward the highway. "I just wish Nick and Peg could get away from their jobs and come for a visit, too."

"Sandi and I were just saying the same thing yesterday," Randi told Mom.

"Our family used to be so close when we all lived out here," Dad said. "After all, it's not that often that a brother and sister from one family gets married to the sister and brother of another family."

10

"It's so romantic," I said with a sigh. "Your older brother marrying Mom's baby sister!"

"Please don't start that romantic stuff," Randi said to me. "Knowing you, you'll be crying in a minute."

"Can I help it if I'm sentimental?" I countered.

About halfway to the airport, Teddy started to get antsy. "I wanna go home," he complained. But no one paid any attention to him. Then he whined his classic car-travel whine. "I gotta go bathroom," he declared. Of course, we all knew he probably didn't have to go, but Mom had to check it out anyway. We just couldn't chance it.

"Do you really, *really* have to go, Teddy?" she asked.

"I gotta go," Teddy insisted. "Now."

But Dad had been fooled by Teddy's little bathroom trick too many times in the past. "If you can wait until we get to the airport," he told Teddy, "I'll buy you an ice-cream cone."

"Ice tream!" Teddy said happily. "I want ice tream. Chock-a-lott ice tream."

"Do you still have to go to the bathroom?" I asked Teddy.

He shook his head. "I want ice tream," he said again.

"You sure outsmarted Teddy that time," Randi said.

"I'm an expert in child psychology," Dad bragged.

"Humph," laughed Mom. "I sure hope so after what you promised Peg and Nick."

"What are you talking about?" I asked Mom.

"Nothing," Mom said. "It's a long story and it doesn't concern you."

I glanced at Randi. She shrugged her shoulders. We were both dying to know what was going on. But from the tone of Mom's voice, we knew better than to ask again.

Three

OF course, Teddy had to have his "ice-tream tone" as soon as we walked through the airport doors. And he was a chocolate mess by the time we headed toward the gate to wait for Mandy's plane.

I took Teddy's hand as we walked along. "Teddy, lick all around the edges," I said to Trouble. "Your ice cream is dripping all over the place."

"Why'd you bother to put good clothes on Teddy?" Randi asked Mom as we trailed after Dad. "Look at him. He's a mess already."

And he was. Chocolate ice cream had dripped out the end of the cone and splattered on the front of his white shirt. And there was ice cream slopped all over his face and arms. Somehow he'd even gotten it in his hair. It grossed me out just to hold his hand.

"We don't have time to get him cleaned up now," Dad said as we entered the waiting area. "Mandy's plane should be here soon."

"Dat was dood," Teddy exclaimed as he crunched on the last bite of his cone.

"Yeah, great," I mumbled as I let go of his sticky hand and inched away from his side. I didn't want anyone to know that this sloppy-looking kid was with me.

Suddenly Dad pointed outside. "That's Mandy's plane now," he said. We all craned our necks to see as a huge jet taxied toward the terminal.

"I can't wait to see Mandy," Mom said eagerly. "I hope I recognize her."

"Me, too," I added.

"Me, three," Randi chimed in.

"How about you, Teddy?" Dad asked. Teddy

didn't answer. "Teddy?" Dad repeated as he turned around. But Teddy wasn't there. "Where's Teddy?" Dad demanded nervously. He frantically began to look around.

"TEDDY!" Mom cried. She nervously looked side to side. "Sandi, where is he?" she asked me.

"He was right here a minute ago," I sputtered.

"He's gone now," Randi exclaimed.

"Oh, no!" Mom cried in alarm. "We've got to find him."

Four

WE looked everywhere, but we couldn't find a trace of Teddy. Once or twice Randi even ran up to someone else's kid, thinking it was Teddy. It was awful! I kept thinking about all the times in the past that I'd told my little brother to get lost. I never really meant it.

"Where should we look now?" Randi asked as we stopped near the escalator.

I glanced up at the balcony of the observation deck. "Let's go up there," I suggested.

We bounded up the escalator and hurried to the railing.

"There he is! Over there by the snack bar!" Randi said, pointing excitedly.

"Yeah!" I hollered. "It is Teddy. He must have wanted another ice-cream cone."

"TEDDY!" Randi shouted, waving her arms. "HEY, TEDDY!" But he didn't hear us.

"Oh, no!" I cried. "There he goes!" We watched in shock as our little brother scooted away again. "Look! He's headed back to where we were supposed to meet Mandy," I announced.

"Let's go," Randi ordered. We raced quickly to the lower level.

Theodore Michael Daniels is a pain sometimes and sometimes he's a lot of trouble. But he's not dumb. He went straight back to where he'd last seen us.

Randi and I got there just in time to see Teddy run toward a young girl who wore an expensive-looking white dress. She was waiting near the gate. When we got a good look at her, we couldn't believe our eyes.

"Hey! Stop! Wait!" the girl in white screamed when she saw an ice cream-covered kid charging toward her. "No! Wait! Don't! Stay away from me, you messy kid!" she yelled.

But that didn't stop Trouble. He buried his chocolate-smeared face into her dress and bearhugged her with sticky, sloppy hands.

"AAURRGGH!" she screeched. "Someone get this icky kid off me!"

But Randi and I didn't move. We couldn't believe what we were seeing. The girl in white looked just like us! It had to be our cousin Mandy. We knew there would be a family resemblance. But we weren't expecting her to look exactly like us. Her hair was a little poofier, but that was about the only difference.

"You must be Mandy," Randi finally managed to say. "Sorry about this." Randi began prying Teddy loose from Mandy.

"Teddy was scared and I guess he thought you were me or Randi," I explained. "He wandered off while we were waiting for you. We were all really worried about him. But everything is fine now."

"Right," Mandy said with anger in her voice.

"Everything is just great. My creepy little cousin just trashed my best dress. And I've never even met him before. Look at me!"

Mandy's dress really was a mess. There were stains and smears all over the front. And on the back Teddy had left two chocolate handprints right across her seat.

"Sorry about your dress, Mandy," I said as I hugged Teddy.

"How could that little brat think I was one of you two?" Mandy continued to rage.

"Listen," Randi snapped. "I let you call my brother a creep because I figured you were upset," she said to Mandy, "but don't call him a brat or anything else again. Understand?"

"Yeah," I butted in. "Don't worry. We'll pay to have your crummy dress cleaned."

"Oh, really? Can you afford it?" Mandy snapped. "I thought you were the poor side of the family."

Randi gritted her teeth. I could tell she was fighting mad.

"Watch it! I know karate," Mandy warned.

"Hey, what's with you two?" I asked. "Remember way back in grade school? We used to be the Three Musketeers. Remember?"

"Three Musketeers is a candy bar," Mandy said in a bored tone.

"Canee," shouted Teddy. "I want canee!"

"Quiet, Teddy," I said. "We have to find Mom and Dad."

"No, we don't," Randi replied. "Here they come now."

"Mom!" I shouted as I saw her and Dad come through the crowd. "We found him!" I turned to look at my stuck-up cousin. "And we found Mandy, too."

"Teddy, you gave us such a scare," Mom said as she rushed up and kissed Trouble. "Thank goodness Randi and Sandi found you."

"Actually, Teddy found Mandy," Randi mumbled as she pointed at our cousin. "And we found them."

"Mandy! It is you!" Mom exclaimed. She

hugged Mandy warmly and kissed her on the cheek.

Mandy smiled in a fake sort of way.

"Mandy, you look so . . . so grown up," Mom continued.

"Hi, Mandy," Dad said. "How was your flight?"

"Miserable," Mandy complained. "There was a lot of turbulence. When I got here, there was no one to meet me. Then my best dress got ruined." She pointed at the stains.

"How did that happen?" Dad asked.

Randi and I pointed at Teddy. He grinned.

Dad sighed and shook his head. "Sorry about that, Mandy," Dad said. "We'll get it cleaned as soon on as we can."

"I can't get over how much you three look alike," Mom said as she stared at Mandy, Randi, and me. "You could be triplets if you all wore your hair the same way."

"I don't think we look *that* much alike," Mandy answered. "Sandi and Randi and I used to . . . before I grew up."

"But we're almost the same age," I quickly added.

"Oh, that's right," Mandy agreed as we walked along. "I forgot. You both just seem so much younger."

Randi glared at Mandy. I hadn't seen her that mad since Roger Perkins called her Moose Face in third grade.

I just kept my mouth shut as we walked to the baggage claim area. I was thinking about what a long summer it was going to be. And I smelled trouble ahead—big trouble. It was more than just double trouble. With Mandy around, I had a feeling we were in for triple trouble.

Five

THINGS didn't get much better after the scene at the airport. First of all, Mandy's luggage ended up on the wrong plane. Her bags were headed to Newark, New Jersey, and Mandy was here with us. I wished it was Mandy who was headed for Newark, New Jersey, instead of her luggage. I could tell from the look on Randi's face that she was thinking the same thing.

We all tried to be cheerful on the way home, but all Mandy could do was complain about her missing luggage and the fact that she'd have to share our clothes. At least she had her precious makeup kit that she had carried on the plane with her. The kit was almost the size of a suitcase!

"Here we are," Dad announced when we pulled into our driveway. "Home sweet home," he said as he parked the car.

"What a charming little house," said Mandy, brightening a little.

"Little? It's one of the biggest houses on the block," Randi corrected.

"I didn't mean that it was small," Mandy snapped. "I meant that it looks cozy."

Randi gave Mandy another one of her looks. I could almost see steam coming out of her ears.

"Everybody out," Dad shouted. "Let's have some lunch. I'm starving."

"Me, too," I added as I nudged Randi.

Randi broke off her staring match with Mandy and opened the door on her side. Mom and Dad got out, too.

Teddy was snoozing on the seat next to me. The long drive home and all the excitement had tired him out. "Wake up, Teddy," I whispered as I shook him gently. "We're home."

Teddy struggled to open his eyes, but he

was just too tired. He looked so adorable asleep like that. At that moment, it was hard to believe that such a sweet little kid could get into so much trouble.

"Let him snooze," Dad told me. "I'll carry him in." Dad leaned into the backseat to pick up Teddy.

"Could you bring in Mandy's makeup kit?" he asked.

I nodded and got out as Dad lifted Teddy and carried him to the house. Mom and Mandy were already on the lawn looking at the flower beds. Randi was holding the front door open for Dad.

I opened the trunk and took out Mandy's makeup kit. It was a big professional makeup kit. I'd never seen anything like it. Every time I want to buy makeup, Mom says I'm too young. But Mandy is only a year older than I am. I wondered what Mom would think of Mandy wearing all this stuff

Dad was coming down the stairs as I walked through the front door. He had put

Teddy down for a nap in his bedroom.

"Where are Mom and Mandy?" I asked.

"They're in the kitchen. Mom's fixing sandwiches for us," Dad said. "And a special salad for Mandy."

"A salad? Why?" I asked.

"Mandy's on a strict diet," Dad explained. "She doesn't want to gain weight."

"Oh," I said, nodding my head. "That figures. Where's Randi?"

Dad jerked his thumb toward the top of the stairs. "She's up in your room looking for a change of clothes for Mandy," he said.

I nodded. "I'll just take Mandy's makeup kit up to our room and I'll be right down," I said. I started up the stairs.

"And tell your sister not to put itching powder in the clothes she picks out, okay?" Dad joked. It hadn't taken Dad long to figure out there was a feud brewing.

I found Randi in our room going through the closet. She pulled out a pair of her jeans and one of my pink blouses. It was my favorite.

"Don't give her that one," I said as I put Mandy's makeup kit on our bed. "Give her my yellow blouse."

"You hate that yellow blouse," Randi replied.

I nodded and grinned. "Oh, I get it," Randi replied as she exchanged the pink blouse for the yellow one.

"Wait," I ordered. "I changed my mind. Give her the pink one." I was mad at Mandy, but I just couldn't bring myself to give her a blouse that I wouldn't wear myself

"Okay," Randi said with a sigh. She switched the blouses again. "It's up to you." Randi walked toward the end. "I wonder what's in there?" she said pointing at the kit.

"I'm dying to find out," I admitted.

Makeup was probably my biggest weakness. I couldn't wait until I was old enough to wear it.

"So let's open it," Randi suggested. "After all, we're sharing our room and our clothes with her. The least she could do is let us sneak a peek."

I looked at the extra bed Dad had put up in our room. I looked at the clothes in Randi's hand. Randi's suggestion did kind of make sense.

"I'll just take a quick look," I said as I snapped open the catch and lifted the lid. "Wow!" I exclaimed. "Would you look at all the stuff!" Mandy's kit was a portable cosmetic counter. There was eyeliner, lipstick, blush, mascara—you name it. She had it all.

"Even Mom doesn't have that much stuff," Randi said.

"Randi! Sandi!" I heard Mom call from downstairs. "Lunch is ready. And bring down that change of clothes for Mandy."

"Coming, Mom," I answered.

"Let's go," Randi urged. "I'm starved. After lunch I want to go to the park and kick around the soccer ball." Randi loved all sports, but soccer was her favorite. It was the one sport I really liked. In fact, we were both goalies on the town team.

"I'll go, too," I said as I turned away from the

kit. "I don't want to be stuck here alone with Mandy."

"It's a good thing we're helping out at the park this summer, or we'd both be stuck with her," Randi said.

When we got to the kitchen, Mandy was just finishing her salad. I couldn't help noticing that she nibbled her lettuce like a rabbit. Every time she chewed, her nose wiggled.

"Here, you can wear these," Randi said as she handed the blouse and jeans to Mandy.

"You expect me to wear these?" Mandi exclaimed in a horrified tone.

"Is something wrong with them?" Randi replied as she took a sandwich from the platter Mom had prepared.

"These jeans aren't in style," Mandy said. "And look at this blouse. I hate pink."

"Well, beggars can't be choosy," I said, picking up my pink blouse. I couldn't hold back my nastiness anymore. "Maybe the color yellow would suit you better. It matches your eyes."

"Girls! Stop that bickering," scolded Mom. "Sandi, I think you owe Mandy an apology."

"That's okay, Aunt Shelly," Mandy interrupted. "I understand. There's no need to apologize. I'm used to people being jealous of me."

"Sandi doesn't have to be jealous of anyone, Mandy," Mom said. "She has plenty going for her."

"But she's not a professional actress like I am," muttered Mandy. "And I can dance, too."

"Do you sing?" I asked, trying to smooth things over.

"Well, no," Mandy admitted.

"Sandi is the lead singer of the school chorus," Randi said as she crunched a potato chip.

"Come on, kids. This isn't a competition," Mom said. "We're all family here."

"You're right, Mom," I agreed. I was getting tired of all this bickering. "Sorry, Mandy."

But Mandy just kind of sighed, took the

blouse and jeans, and went upstairs to change. Randi looked at me and rolled her eyes.

Dad came in and eyed the platter of sandwiches. "Good! Lunch at last," Dad said as he picked one up.

But before he even had a chance to take a bite, a piercing shriek echoed through the house.

"That scream came from our room," I said as we all ran upstairs.

A second scream made us move even faster. Randi and I reached the open doorway to our room at the same time. Our jaws dropped open when we saw what was going on.

"What is it?" Mom asked as she and Dad came up behind us. "What's wrong?"

Mandy was shaking in a fit of anger and staring at my bed. Teddy, who was now wide awake, was sitting on the bed. Next to him was Mandy's makeup kit. It was completely empty. Teddy had gotten into everything. Mandy's bed was covered with splotches of blush and

streaks of lipstick. Mascara was on the sheets and pillowcases. The room looked like someone had set off a makeup bomb in it. And Teddy? He was grinning. Colored blotches were all over his face.

"I a clown," Teddy said.

"Look at what that little monster did!" Mandy yelled, grabbing her kit. "He ruined all my makeup."

Mom walked into our room. She put her arms around Mandy and tried to make her feel better. But Mandy just kept getting madder and madder.

"I want that kid punished," she ordered. "Spank him. Put him in a corner. Do something!"

"Sorry, Mandy," Dad said. "We don't use those kinds of punishment around here. Besides, Teddy didn't know he was doing anything wrong. He was just playing."

"It was an accident," I chimed in.

"That was a *professional* makeup kit," sputtered Mandy, tears welling up in her eyes.

"A professional actress needs her makeup. What will I do without it?"

"What makes you think you're such a big shot actress, anyway?" Randi said. She was losing her temper in a big way. "You're just a no-talent model. You can't even sing."

For a second Mandy didn't say anything. Then she blew up. "I didn't want to come here in the first place," she said. "I knew something like this would happen. My parents made me come. I hate it here already."

"Whoa, everybody, just ice down or cool out—whatever it is they say today," Dad said.

"Chill out," I said.

"Okay, now chill out," Dad instructed. "We *are* going to spend this summer together and we *are* going to get along."

"Sandi, you and Randi take Teddy to the bathroom and get him cleaned up," Dad ordered. "Shell, you and I will help Mandy save what we can from her kit," he said to Mom. He looked at Mandy. "But Mandy, I think you're too young to be wearing all that makeup anyway."

"I agree," Mom added. Mandy frowned.

"Let's go, clownie," I said to Teddy as Randi and I dragged him down the hall to the bathroom.

Six

RANDI and I cleaned up Teddy, and then we went back downstairs. Mandy stayed upstairs pouting. Dad was sitting alone at the kitchen table, finishing his lunch.

"Sit down," he said. "I want to talk to you girls about Mandy." Randi sighed loudly as we both pulled up chairs.

"This isn't all our fault, Dad," I said. "Mandy isn't easy to get along with."

"And she started most of it," Randi added.

Dad waved his hand in the air. "I know," he admitted. "In some ways I agree with you one hundred percent."

Boy, were we ever shocked. We'd expected to

get bawled out and here Dad was agreeing with us. Randi looked at me. I looked at her. Randi shrugged her shoulders, and decided to stretch her luck.

"Are you saying that you think Mandy is a spoiled brat, too?" Randi asked.

"Well, in a way," Dad said.

"Are you saying you don't like Mandy, either?" I asked.

"I didn't say that," Dad explained. "Mandy has some problems. She's spoiled. She's conceited. And she thinks she's older than she is."

"That just about says it," Randi agreed.

"But she is my niece. And she's your cousin. And you used to be good friends," Dad continued.

"That was a long time ago," Randi said.

"But she's family," he went on, "and she has some problems I think we can help her with."

"I still don't like her," Randi grumbled.

I thought for a minute. "How can you say that, Randi?" I asked.

"Easy," she said.

"But Randi, don't you see?" I asked. "It's like hating me or yourself. Mandy really is almost like our sister," I said.

Randi sighed. Then she put an elbow on the table and put her chin in her hand. She knew I was right. Down deep you care about your relatives no matter how obnoxious they are. And Mandy is a very, very close relative. I knew down deep that Randi felt the same way I did about our cousin.

"Now I'm going to tell you something that I don't want you to tell anyone else," Dad continued. "Mandy's visiting here for a reason. Uncle Nick and Aunt Peg are very concerned about Mandy. They asked your mother and me for our help."

"Help?" Randi asked, surprised.

"Yes," Dad went on, "but I'm only telling you this because of the way things are going. You have to promise not to tell Mandy."

I looked at my sister. "I promise," I said.

After a short silence Randi said, "I promise too."

"Okay," said Dad. "I'll spill the beans. Uncle Nick and Aunt Peg think that Mandy is caught up in too much Hollywood glitter. She's trying to grow up too fast. She has no friends or interests other than her acting career. And that can be hard on a person."

Randi and I nodded.

"Because she is an only child, Mandy is spoiled," Dad went on. "That's why she thinks she's the most important person in the world."

"I think I see what you mean, Dad," I said. "Mandy has never had to share with anyone. She's never been part of a big family."

"I get it," Randi said. "She's supposed to learn how to live with other kids by spending the summer with us.

"Right," Dad answered. "You two are supposed to be a good influence on Mandy. You're going to teach her how to act her own age."

"We haven't done such a good job so far, have we?" I asked, glancing at Randi.

"Well, tomorrow's another day," Dad said as he smiled at us.

"But we start our volunteer work at the recreation program tomorrow," Randi said.

"I know," Dad replied. "So take Mandy with you."

Randi groaned. I felt like groaning, too! Taking Mandy with us was a lot to ask. But it was the right thing to do. I nudged Randi with my elbow. "Oh, come on," I urged. Randi still didn't answer.

"Oh, okay," Randi agreed.

"Great," I said. I looked at Dad. "We'll try our best, Dad," I promised.

"But I don't think it's going to be easy," Randi added.

I agreed with Randi on that one. It definitely would not be easy.

Seven

MAKING up with Mandy that night was one of the hardest things we ever had to do. Of course, we did all of the apologizing. And the next morning was even worse. Mandy didn't want to get up early to go to the rec program with us. She took two hours in the bathroom getting ready, and then left the sink and floor a mess. Then she moaned and groaned through breakfast. Because of her special diet, she said she had to have a poached egg. Cold cereal sounded better to Randi and me.

"Hurry up. We'll be late," Randi complained as she held open the front door for Mandy and me.

"I don't see why I have to go along," Mandy

whined. "I'd rather stay here."

"Dad wants you to," I said. "And we want you to," I quickly added.

"Do I look all right?" Mandy asked. She was dressed in one of Randi's outfits.

"You look fine," I said as we walked along. She did look fine. In fact, she looked a lot like Randi. She might even have looked a little better than Randi.

"Come on!" Randi ordered, urging us to move faster.

"What's the big rush?" Mandy wanted to know.

"I've got things to do," Randi answered. "I've got to get the soccer balls out of the field house. And I've got to help put the nets on the goals at the field."

Randi's job was working with Coach Matthews.

"And I have to help Miss Morgan put out the paints and things for arts and crafts," I added.

"How exciting," Mandy said in a bored tone. "Is it much farther to your school?"

"Nah, not far," I said as we turned a corner.

"Uh-oh," Randi muttered, stopping short. "Look over there," she said to me. "Do you see who I see?"

I squinted as I looked down the block. I still wasn't used to my new contact lenses. Up ahead I saw a girl on a bike. She was stuffing newspapers into a newspaper bag. It was Bobbi Joy Boikin. She loved to scare people. Randi and I were about the only two people in school who didn't bow to her. And that really bugged Bobbi Joy.

"Let's cross the street," Randi suggested.

"Why?" Mandy wondered out loud. We didn't explain. We just took her by the arms and led her to the other side.

And it was just in time. Bobbi Joy came tearing down the sidewalk on the other side of the street. "Hey, why did the chickens cross the road?" she yelled at us as she pedaled past. "Because they saw Bobbi Joy coming!" she mocked.

"Who is that?" Mandy asked.

"It's Bobbi Joy Boikin," Randi explained. "She's always trying to scare Sandi and me. We just avoid her whenever we can."

Mandy nodded. "I'm not afraid of bullies," Mandy bragged. "I take karate lessons," she said, taking a karate stance.

"Yeah, you told us once before," I reminded her, "at the airport."

"Oh, right," Mandy mumbled as we approached the school where the rec program was held in the summer.

"Wow!" Mandy shouted. "Who's that hunk over there?" She pointed at a blond boy who was sitting near the soccer field.

Randi and I glanced at each other. "She would spot him right off," Randi whispered to me.

"At least she has good taste," I whispered back.

Mandy turned toward us. "What are you two mumbling about? Do you know his name or not?"

I nodded. "His name is Christopher Miles," I said. "He's new. He moved here at the end of the school year. He's a really good student."

"And a great athlete," Randi added.

"He's gorgeous," Mandy sighed as she watched Chris and his younger brother.

"I guess he's all right," Randi admitted. "He's not a nerd or anything."

"He seems very nice," I said to Mandy. "We'd both like to get to know him better. But we haven't had the chance yet. We really could use him on our soccer team."

Mandy laughed. "Well, you missed your chance. It's my turn now," she said. "Meeting him might make this trip worthwhile after all."

Mandy looked at Randi. Then she looked at me. A sly smile spread across her lips, showing her perfectly straight teeth. "Christopher Miles," she purred. "What a nice name."

As Randi headed for the soccer field, she said, "He's not your type, Mandy."

"Touchy, isn't she?" Mandy said after Randi had left. Then Mandy looked at me and laughed. That laugh worried me. I wondered what sneaky plot my cousin was cooking up.

Eight

WHEN I introduced Mandy to Miss Morgan, she couldn't believe how much Mandy looked like Randi and me.

"You two look so much alike it's like having double vision," Miss Morgan said as she looked at Mandy and me standing side by side. "But she does look a little more like Randi, if that's possible."

"That's only because Mandy is wearing Randi's clothes today," I told Miss Morgan. "If she was dressed in my clothes, she'd look more like me."

Mandy kind of frowned through the whole conversation.

"Maybe you're right," Miss Morgan agreed.

Then we got busy putting out the things for arts and crafts. It was almost time for the little kids to start showing up. The day's arts and crafts project was going to be fingerpainting. Mandy stood around and watched as Miss Morgan and I did all the work. She never offered to help.

Soon little boys and girls started to fill up the tables. Miss Morgan and I began opening jars of fingerpaint for the kids to paint with. Now that the work was done and the fun was beginning, Mandy suddenly wanted to help. She came rushing up to help me with a jar of paint that I was having trouble opening.

"Let me get that for you," Mandy offered. She sat next to me and twisted the top with all her might. But when she spun the lid off, she moved her arm closer to me. Splat! Slop! Paint splattered over my blouse and shorts.

"Look what you did!" I shouted. "You did that on purpose!"

"Oh, no! It was an accident, really," Mandy insisted as she put the jar down. "But you'd

51

better go wash it off before it dries."

"Thanks for the advice," I said as I turned and walked toward the school building behind us.

When I got to the restroom, I peeked out the window at Mandy. Chris Miles and his little brother were walking toward her. No wonder Mandy wanted me out of the way. She wanted to be alone with Chris!

"Uh, Randi?" I heard Chris say to Mandy. "It is you, isn't it?"

"Of course I'm Randi," Mandy lied. I saw her flash him a big smile.

I tried to stifle a gasp from my hiding place by the window. But what could I do? I couldn't let Chris see me like this. I looked like a real slob, all covered with paint.

"You . . . you look a little different, that's all," I heard Chris say.

"Different better or different worse?" Mandy wanted to know.

"Different older," he explained. "I—I guess I never saw you with makeup on before."

I could tell from Chris's stuttering that he was nervous. Then his little brother, Carl, who'd been silently standing beside him, nudged him with his elbow.

"Tell her," Carl said. "Come on, tell her!"

"Oh, yeah," Chris sputtered. "I want to thank you for teaching my little brother how to dribble."

"Huh?" I heard Mandy say. She was going to have to be pretty sharp to get out of this one, I thought to myself.

"You know in the park . . . last week?" Chris asked. "Remember? You showed Carl how to dribble a soccer ball."

"Oh . . . oh, yeah! Sure," Mandy said. "Your brother is a natural."

"I want to go fingerpaint now," Carl told his older brother.

"Sure. Go ahead," Chris said as Carl went over to the table where Miss Morgan was working with several other kids.

For a second or two I watched Chris and

Mandy stare at each other. "Could you teach me?" Chris asked, breaking the silence. "I love soccer. I want to play on the team next season."

Mandy didn't answer.

"Well, can you? I mean . . . will you?" Chris asked again.

"Will I what?" Mandy asked.

"Teach me to dribble," Chris clarified.

"Sure. No problem. Anytime. When it comes to soccer, I know it all," Mandy said.

"Great. My ball's right over there," Chris said. "How about showing me a couple of pointers right now?"

How's Mandy going to get out of this one? I wondered. "Let's walk away from the building," she suggested. "We don't want to bother anyone here."

When I came out of the building after getting my shirt cleaned off, I saw just how Mandy was planning to wangle her way out of her lies.

Mandy was hobbling toward the school with her arm around Chris's shoulder. She had one

leg off the ground as if she had hurt it. Even though I'd only been with her a day, I could tell she was acting. I had to hand it to Mandy in a way, though. She sure had managed to get herself out of a difficult situation.

I was straining to hear what she was saying—something about an old sports injury—when Jamie Collins, my best friend from school, walked toward me.

"That must be your cousin, Mandy, the one from Hollywood," Jamie said, nodding toward the bench where Chris and Mandy were now sitting. "I almost thought it was Randi for a minute." Jamie was one of the few people who knew Randi and me well enough to tell us apart most of the time.

"Yeah! That's cousin Mandy the actress," I grunted.

"She sure didn't waste any time meeting Chris," Jamie said.

I frowned. "Chris sure looks like he's enjoying the attention," I grumbled. "I guess he's just another goofy boy after all."

"I don't know," Jamie said, disagreeing. "He seems to be pretty smart. He reads almost as much as you do. Maybe he's just being polite."

I looked at Jamie. Then I looked at Chris and Mandy sitting on the bench. "I don't think so," I muttered.

"Sandi, I need you," Miss Morgan called.

"Coming," I answered as I glared at Mandy. "I'll get you back, Mandy," I mumbled as I walked away. "Some way, some how, I'll get you back!"

Nine

"YOU'RE stuck with Mandy today," I said to Randi as we got ready to leave the next morning.

"Yeah, but today she's wearing your clothes," Randi retorted.

"I can always throw out the clothes later," I said, giggling. I hadn't told Randi about Mandy's little acting routine on the soccer field. The two of them were having enough problems, I figured.

"I'm ready to go to work," Mandy announced as she pranced down the stairs past Teddy, who was playing in the hall.

"Bye, Sanee," Teddy said to Mandy.

"Did you hear that?" Randi asked me.

"Trouble thinks Mandy is you."

"Don't rub it in," I told my sister as Mandy came up to us.

"Hurry up," Mandy urged. "We don't want to be late." She opened the door.

"What's with her?" Randi asked as we went out.

"Come on," Mandy said as she hurried down the walk. We quickly caught up with her.

"Hey!" I said, noticing something different about Mandy. "You're not wearing makeup today."

"A girl doesn't need makeup to look pretty," she replied.

Randi gave me a puzzled look.

With Mandy leading the way, we got to school extra early.

"I have to give the coach a hand putting up the nets," Randi said to Mandy when we got to the school. "Want to help?"

"I would," Mandy answered as she held up a hand, "but I might break a nail."

Randi rolled her eyes and left Mandy in the same spot she'd been in yesterday, under the tree right next to the girls' rest room.

Seconds later, Chris Miles came walking up with his brother. I could tell from the gleam in Mandy's eyes that she was up to something. And the best way to figure it out, I thought, was to listen in the way I had yesterday.

I grabbed the jar of fingerpaint with the stubborn lid and told Miss Morgan that I was going to open it over the sink to avoid any more disasters. Then I quietly entered the rest room and assumed my position next to the open window.

Just seconds after I got settled in my spot, Chris Miles came walking up with his brother.

"Hello, Christopher," Mandy said.

"Oh, hi . . . Sandi?" Chris sputtered. "I didn't see you there by that tree. It is Sandi, isn't it? You look different since school ended. You don't wear your glasses anymore."

I listened again as Mandy followed Chris's

lead. Only this time, he thought she was me. So Mandy played along. Believe me, it was tough standing there listening when Mandy was playing her little game. I was getting madder every second.

"Do you like me better with glasses or without?" Mandy asked, flashing Chris a smile.

"It doesn't matter," he said. "'I like you both ways."

"I like you, too," Mandy replied.

"Come on, Chris," Carl said. "I came early so I could practice extra dribbling."

"Okay," Chris said. "I want to check and make sure Randi's ankle is okay today." He turned to Mandy. "She hurt it trying to show me how to dribble."

"I know," Mandy replied. "Her ankle is fine today. See!" She pointed out to the middle of the field. Randi and Coach Matthews were bringing the balls out of the field house. Randi was dribbling two balls at once. "Go on out there, Carl," Mandy urged. "Randi will be happy to work with you."

Carl didn't need to be told twice. He shot out on the field and raced over to Randi.

"I heard you're pretty good at soccer, too, Sandi," Chris said to Mandy.

Mandy nodded, playing along. I stood by the window with my blood boiling!

"And you read a lot, too," Chris continued.

"Do you read a lot?" Mandy asked.

"I love to read," Chris admitted. "What's your favorite book?"

"My favorite book?" Mandy mumbled, trying to think of an answer. I figured that the only things she ever read were movie magazines.

"My favorite book is *The Adventures of Tom Sawyer*," Chris admitted.

"It's my favorite, too," Mandy agreed quickly.

"Samuel Clemens was some writer," Chris went on.

"Samuel Clemens? I thought Mark Twain wrote Tom Sawyer," Mandy said.

I had to bite my cheeks to keep from

laughing. Mandy didn't even know that Samuel Clemens was Mark Twain. Chris was going to catch her in her lie now! I couldn't wait to hear more.

But Chris just laughed. "You and your sister have great senses of humor," Chris said. "Of course you know Mark Twain is Samuel Clemens's pen name."

"Of course," Mandy agreed. "I should have known I couldn't trick you. What book are you reading now?"

"*The Time Machine* by H. G. Wells," Chris answered. "Have you ever read it?"

"No. Tell me about it," Mandy suggested, and the two of them walked off together. Mandy the actress had done it again!

Ten

AS the summer went on, some days Mandy dressed like me and some days she dressed like Randi. And no matter who she was dressed like, every time I turned around she was spending time with Chris Miles. She really had some crush on him. And somehow she always worked it so he never saw the three of us together.

Of course, Mom and Dad were just thrilled about the way things were going. To them, Mandy seemed like a changed girl. She'd quit wearing makeup. She seemed to enjoy wearing our clothes. She was even styling her hair more like ours. They figured we were a good influence on her. But they didn't know the truth.

"Mandy acts more and more like you two every day," Mom said to Randi and me one evening while Mandy was in the shower. "It's almost like Mandy is studying you to learn how to act around other kids her age," Mom continued. "I didn't think things were going to work out this summer, but they are." And she went out of the room.

I sat there thinking. I glanced at Mandy's baggage, which had finally arrived from the airport. It was on the floor near Mandy's bed, still unpacked. Mandy no longer wanted to wear her own clothes. She insisted on wearing ours day after day. I had a feeling that Mandy was pulling the switcheroo trick with Chris whenever she could. She sure was avoiding Chris Miles when the three of us were together.

"What's with you?" Randi asked. Randi could tell that I was thinking about something serious. "Are you sick or something?"

"Kind of," I replied. "You know, we've both been wondering why Chris Miles is spending so much time with Mandy and completely ignoring us," I said, thinking hard.

"Yeah!"

"Well, suppose he thinks Mandy isn't Mandy."

"Huh?" Randi grunted.

"Suppose," I continued, "he thinks Mandy is one of us."

"You mean the switch routine we pulled that one time?" Randi asked.

"Yup," I said. "I'll bet she's been pretending to be you or me whenever it does her good."

"I'll bet you're right," Randi agreed. "But how can we prove it? She'll never own up to it. We'll have to get proof, catch her red-handed."

"I have caught her red-handed a couple of times," I said, and I explained to Randi about the two times I'd caught Mandy in the act at the school.

"Why didn't you do anything?" Randi demanded. "Why didn't you say anything to her? Or me?"

"Things were going so well," I answered.

"And I didn't think she'd be able to keep the whole thing up for very long. Boy, was I wrong!"

"Were you ever," Randi sighed. "We've just got to find a way to nab her—and soon. Who knows what she's saying to Chris when she's pretending to be us!"

Before we could think any further, the phone rang. It was Jamie Collins.

"Are you going to the rec dance Monday night?" Jamie asked me when I answered the phone.

"I don't know. Why?" I asked.

"I think you should," Jamie continued. "I'm going. And Chris Miles is going. His mom was just here, and she told me he hopes he'll see both you and Randi there."

Chris Miles lived right next door to Jamie Collins. In fact, their mothers were becoming very good friends.

"How about Mandy?" I asked.

"That's the strangest thing," Jamie continued. "Chris's mom never even mentioned Mandy

once. I don't think she knows Mandy exists."

"You know, I don't think Christopher knows Mandy exists either," I replied.

"Huh?" Jamie said sounding confused. Then I explained what had been going on.

"So that's it," Jamie said. "I thought there was something fishy about Mandy. What are you going to do about it?"

"I think," I began, "Randi and I will be going to the rec dance at school Monday night. It sounds like the perfect time to get Mandy back."

"Can I be part of the fun?" Jamie asked.

"Sure," I replied. "In fact, you can be a big help. Do you think you can arrange for Randi and me to meet with Christopher later today?"

"Sure. We can meet at the school around three o'clock."

"Right."

I hung up the phone and smiled. I couldn't wait to get cooking on our plan.

Eleven

"**D**O you think Chris will help us?" Randi asked me as we rode our bikes over to the school to meet with Chris and Jamie.

"I'm sure he will," I answered. "When he hears about the trick Mandy played, he'll be boiling mad."

"I was," Randi admitted as we approached the back of the school where Jamie and Chris were waiting.

"Hi, Sandi. Hi, Randi," Jamie called as our bikes came to a stop.

"Hi, Sandi and Randi," echoed Chris. "What's this all about? Jamie insisted I come over here but wouldn't tell me why. What's the big mystery?" Chris looked at me. "You didn't mention anything about this earlier today when we went to the library."

I walked closer to Chris. "Maybe I'm not the same person I was earlier today," I said. Jamie and Randi giggled.

"What's so funny about that?" Chris asked.

"Do I look different?" I asked.

Chris studied me for a minute. "You do look a little different," he admitted. "Your hair isn't exactly the same, and there are other little things I can't really explain."

"I can explain them," Randi said. "The person you were with this morning wasn't Sandi."

Chris looked at her as if she'd gone bonkers.

"Huh?" was all he could say.

"It really wasn't me, Chris," I said.

"Don't tell me," Chris chuckled. "It was a robot that looks and acts human."

That made me laugh. I figured I'd better tell Chris the whole story. "You've been spending time with our cousin Mandy."

"Your cousin Mandy?" he sputtered. "Who's she?"

"She's a hotshot actress from Hollywood who thinks she's a big deal," Randi explained.

Chris was now more confused than ever.

"Our cousin looks so much like us that we could pass for triplets," I continued. "She wanted to meet you. And she wanted to play a dirty trick on us. So she pretended to be Randi or me whenever she could. I guess she thinks it's a real joke!"

Chris scratched his head and thought for a minute. "You know, all this crazy stuff you're telling me kind of makes sense. You—I mean she always does act sort of funny as if she doesn't know exactly what to do or say. I thought she was just shy."

"Well I don't think any of this is funny at all," Randi grunted.

"Yeah," Chris snapped. "I wonder how Mandy would feel if someone played a trick like that on her!"

"I wonder . . . ," I said, grinning from ear to ear.

Chris' eyes brightened. "Do you have something in mind?"

"Do we ever," I chuckled.

"What do I have to do?" Chris wanted to know.

"First, we have to get you to meet cousin Mandy as cousin Mandy," I said.

"How do I do that?" Chris asked.

"Jamie will bring you over to our house tomorrow," Randi explained. "We'll arrange for Mandy to be outside. Mandy wouldn't dare pretend to be Sandi or me in front of Jamie. She'll have to be herself."

"Right," I agreed. "She's smart enough to know she couldn't fool Jamie."

"What then?" Chris wanted to know.

"Then you pretend that Mandy is the neatest girl you ever saw," I continued. "And you ask her to the rec dance on Monday night."

"You mean like a date?" Chris sputtered. "A real date? My parents won't like that. I'm too young for a real date."

"It's not like a real date," I explained. "All

you have to do is pick up Mandy at our house, walk her to the rec dance, and we'll do the rest."

"Tell me more about the rest," urged Chris.

I smiled and whispered our plan into his ear. When I finished, he was grinning a wide grin.

"I'll do it!" Chris announced eagerly as he shook my hand.

Twelve

THE next afternoon was hot and sunny. Even the weather was cooperating with our plan. We convinced Mandy to sunbathe out in the backyard alone so Jamie could introduce her to Chris. And it didn't take much convincing to get Mandy to go outside. We told her she could either sunbathe or help us clean our room.

"I think I'll do some sunbathing," Mandy said as she opened her suitcase for the first time and sifted through her things, looking for a bathing suit. She quickly dressed and put on a pair of dark sunglasses. "I'm going outside now," she announced.

We put the lounge chair for Mandy near one

of the rear windows of the house. With the window open, we'd be able to overhear every word.

After Mandy stretched out on the lounge and got comfortable, we rushed inside and phoned Jamie Collins. She and Chris were just waiting for our signal.

Before long, Jamie and Chris arrived on their bikes. Randi and I peeked out of the window to see what was going to happen.

When Mandy saw Chris, she sat up stiffly. She looked like she was going to make a mad dash for the house but Jamie quickly called to her before she could move.

"Hi, Mandy," Jamie shouted. "Don't run away. There's someone here I want you to meet."

"Oh, hi, Jamie," Mandy gulped.

"Chris, this is Mandy Rogers," Jamie said. "She's Sandi and Randi's cousin from Hollywood, California. Mandy is an actress. She was even in a TV commercial."

"Wow!" said Chris, pretending to be really

impressed. "That's super. I never met a TV star before," he said, wide-eyed.

"Boy, is he ever laying it on thick," I whispered to Randi as we peered through the window screen.

Mandy lifted her sunglasses and smiled one of her fake smiles. "I'm pleased to meet you, too, Chris," she said. She still wasn't sure he didn't recognize her.

Chris went right on with his act. "Is it exciting to live in Hollywood?" Chris asked.

Mandy nodded slowly.

"It's boring living around here," Chris continued. "I never meet anyone interesting . . . like you."

"What about Randi and Sandi?" Mandy said.

"Yeah, what about them?" Jamie asked. She looked sternly at Chris and then winked.

"Oh, they're all right. But they're just plain, ordinary girls," Chris said. This comment made us cover our mouths and snicker. "They're not glamorous like you."

"They're not so plain and ordinary," Mandy countered. We couldn't believe our ears. Mandy was actually sticking up for us. Maybe she really wasn't so rotten after all. "My cousins are very nice people. And they're cute, too."

"I know, I know," Chris agreed. "It's just that I never met anyone as talented as you are before. I hear that you dance—and sing, too."

"I'm a good dancer," Mandy said. "I've had years of lessons. But I can't sing a note. I have one of the worst voices of all time."

"But you dance," Chris said. "Hey, that reminds me. There's a recreation dance Monday night. Why don't we go together?" Chris asked.

Mandy paused. "I'm not sure. Maybe I'd better go with my cousins."

"They're not going," Jamie quickly said.

"How do you know?" Mandy asked.

"They told me," Jamie replied. "They both hate dances."

"Oh," said Mandy. "I guess it would be all right then."

"It'll be great," Jamie shouted. "You'll finally get a chance to meet all the kids in the neighborhood."

"Great!" Chris said to Mandy. "I'll come over here Monday night, and we'll walk to the dance together."

Mandy nodded.

"Where are the twins?" Jamie asked Mandy.

"They're up in their room," Mandy answered.

"I'll go up," Jamie said. She turned to Chris. "Coming?"

Chris got on his bike. "No," he replied. "I'm going to go tell everyone I'm taking a movie star to the dance." And he rode off as fast as he could.

Mandy looked at Jamie. Jamie shrugged her shoulders and went into the house. We met her at the back door. We patted each other on the back and giggled like crazy. Our plan was going perfectly!

Thirteen

MOM was really pleased when Mandy announced at dinner that Chris was taking her to the recreation dance. I guess she felt Mandy was finally being accepted in the neighborhood. After all, she didn't seem to be making any friends until then. Of course Mom didn't know that the reason she wasn't making any friends was because she was too busy pretending to be Randi or me.

But Mandy seemed more concerned about what Randi and I thought about her date for the dance than about getting Mom and Dad's permission to go. And of course they gave it.

"Sandi, you and Randi aren't mad about me

going with Chris, are you?" Mandy asked.

"Why should we be mad?" I answered.

"Yeah, why should we be mad?" Randi echoed. "We don't like dances anyway. We're not even going."

Mandy shrugged her shoulders. Something seemed to be bothering her. "May I be excused?" she asked.

"I'm finished," I added. "May I go, too?"

"Me, too," Randi said, dabbing her napkin against her lips.

Dad nodded. We all started to get up.

"I done," Teddy exclaimed as he started to slide off his chair.

"Hold it, young man," Dad ordered. "Finish your peas."

"Yuck," we heard Teddy groan as we started up the stairs to our room.

Randi and I went in first. Mandy walked in after us. "You're sure you don't mind about Chris?" she asked again. "I won't go if you don't want me to."

That didn't sound like Mandy. She sure was acting funny.

"Oh, we want you to go," Randi urged. "We really, really want you to go to the dance."

"Chris is just another friend," I said. "We understand if he likes you. We'd kind of guessed that he did. After all, he's been spending all that time with you at the rec activities."

Randi chimed in. "Yeah, that's right."

"And once he really got to know *you* well," I continued, "I guess he started liking *you* a lot." Every time I said the word "you," I really emphasized it.

Mandy flopped on her bed. She really looked upset.

"So what's the problem?" I asked.

Mandy sighed. "To tell the truth," she confessed, "hardly anyone ever likes the real me. Back in California I have an agent, a dance teacher, and an acting coach, but no friends. I just don't make friends easily. I'm always too busy with lessons or auditions."

Randi glanced at me and raised her eyebrows. I shrugged.

"That's why I can't understand why Chris asked me instead of you, Sandi, or you, Randi," Mandy continued. "I guess that's why I like acting so much. It gives me a chance to be somebody else instead of myself. Sometimes I think I'd rather be you two than me."

"Why in the world would you say that?" I asked. "Your life is so glamorous."

"But you have each other," Mandy explained. "I wish I had a sister."

She got off her bed and started for the hall bathroom. When she was gone, I turned to Randi. Maybe we had her all wrong. Before I could speak, Randi cut me off.

"Forget it, Miss Sentimental," she said. "I was touched by all that stuff too, but we're going through with the plan."

"But Randi . . . ," I said.

"No buts. No matter what the reason, it was a rotten thing that Mandy did," Randi continued.

"And she still hasn't confessed to it."

"You're right," I agreed. "We owe it to ourselves and we owe it to Mandy to teach her a lesson."

"The plan is on?" Randi asked.

"It's on!" I agreed and gave my sister a thumbs-up sign.

Fourteen

ON Monday evening, Mandy actually seemed jittery as she dressed for the dance. Since she was going to the dance as herself, she didn't need to borrow any of our clothes. And this time, we studied Mandy's every move. We especially paid close attention to the way she did her hair.

"Do you two have to stare at me like that?" Mandy asked as she checked herself in the mirror.

"Sorry, we didn't mean to," I apologized. I had to admit that she really did look beautiful when she dressed up. I couldn't help but be impressed.

Mandy added a few finishing touches to her hair. I went over and lay on my bed so I was on

my stomach facing her. I wanted to make sure I got a good look at her hair. Randi stared and studied, too.

Just then the doorbell rang.

"Chris Miles is here," Mom announced, opening the door to our room. Then she looked at Mandy. "You look beautiful, dear," Mom complimented. "Those jeans and that sweater are lovely. You really do have such nice clothes."

"Thank you," said Mandy. "This sweater is special. I bought it at a designer shop with the money I made from the commercial I did."

Mom nodded. "Hurry up," she instructed. "Chris is waiting downstairs."

Mandy turned toward us. "Bye," she said. "See you later."

"Yes, see you later," Randi replied with a grin.

"Bye," I said as Mom and Mandy went out. When they were gone I hopped off the bed. I went to the door and peeked down the hall. It was all clear. "It's okay," I said to Randy. "Let's get dressed."

Randi and I giggled as we dressed. "We may not be able to wear the exact same clothes as Mandy," Randi said, "but we sure can duplicate the way she does her hair."

I nodded. "Thank goodness she doesn't wear all that makeup anymore. Mom would never let us out of the house like that."

"As soon as we're dressed," Randi said. "I'll tell Dad we decided to go to the dance after all. I'm sure it'll be okay."

When Randi and I got to the school building, the dance was well underway. Music was blaring. The band onstage was really good. Some kids were milling around the refreshment stand. Most were dancing. Jamie Collins was waiting for us at the side entrance to the gym as we had planned.

"Where are they?" I asked Jamie.

Jamie didn't answer. She just stared at us in awe. "I can't believe it," she said in an amazed tone. "You two really look just like Mandy. I mean . . . she looks like you. I mean . . . you all look alike."

Randi and I smiled. "You sure have a way with words, Jamie," Randi kidded.

"But it's scary," Jamie gulped. "You're all dressed a little different, yet you're all identical. It's like seeing triple."

"Well, that is the plan," I reminded Jamie as I smoothed my hair. "Now to repeat my question. Where are they? We have to make sure Mandy doesn't see us."

"Oh, sorry," apologized Jamie. "Chris is keeping Mandy near the refreshment stand just like he's supposed to. She doesn't suspect a thing."

"Did you talk to Coach Matthews and Miss Morgan?" Randi asked.

Jamie nodded. "They'd love to have you, I mean Mandy perform. But you'll have to talk with them in person first."

"Well, let's go talk to them right now," I said to Jamie.

"While you're doing that, I'll circulate around the guys," Randi said. "They'll think I'm Mandy, so I'll arrange to dance with all of them at once.

I'm sure they'd be more than interested in dancing with Mandy the movie star, especially since Chris bragged about her to every guy in town."

"Oh, I'm sure they will," Jamie assured Randi. "Mandy's kind of the hit of the dance. The guys can hardly keep their eyes off her."

"Just make sure you set her up to dance with all of the guys here," I told Randi. "After all, we want cousin Mandy to enjoy herself."

"Don't worry, I will," Randi promised as she moved off into the crowded gymnasium.

"Now, let's go," I said to Jamie. "It's time to begin Operation Triple Trouble."

Jamie and I went into the gym and made our way over to Coach Matthews and Miss Morgan. They were the chaperones of the dance.

"Here she is," Jamie announced. "Mandy Rogers, the famous Hollywood actress."

"Nice to see you again," Miss Morgan said.

"I'm pleased to meet you, Mandy," Coach Matthews greeted. He studied me closely. "I heard you look a lot like Randi and Sandi, but now that we meet, I don't think you do."

Jamie giggled a little at that comment.

"I'm pleased to meet you too, Coach," I said. "I heard you're an excellent softball coach."

"Uh, not softball, soccer," he corrected.

"Oh, yes, right, of course," I teased.

"Mandy, are you sure you want to sing in front of this large crowd?" Miss Morgan asked. "Jamie said you wouldn't mind. I just wanted to check to be sure."

"Oh no! I don't mind at all," I said. "I'd love it. Singing is my life. It would be a great thrill for me to sing at this dance."

"Super," Miss Morgan said. Miss Morgan always said "super." It was her pet word. I guess it was an "in" word to use when she was young. "I'll arrange it with the band," Miss Morgan continued. "It will be a nice added attraction. Where can I find you later?" Miss Morgan asked.

"I'll be by the refreshment stand," I said as we walked away. When we were out of hearing distance, Jamie and I burst out laughing. We leaned back against a wall, covered our faces with our hands, and giggled until tears filled our eyes.

"What's so funny?" someone asked. "Did you look in a mirror?"

We stopped laughing and looked up. There in front of us was Bobbi Joy Boikin, acting tough, as usual.

"Do you want something, Bobbi?" Jamie asked.

Bobbi sneered and grunted. "I want little Miss Hollywood here to stay away from my boyfriend." Bobbi Joy pointed a finger at me.

Oh no! Bobbi Joy thought I was Mandy, too!

"Wh-What do you mean?" I asked.

"Todd Jackson! He's with me!" Bobbi Joy continued. "I saw you talk with those other boys. Dance with them if you want. But leave Todd alone." And she lumbered away with her teeth clenched.

"Randi must really be getting around the

gym," I said to Jamie. "But Todd 'the Cod' Jackson? YUCK!"

Todd the Cod Jackson always did rude things like burping out loud in class. He was a totally gross kid. Bobbi Joy and Todd the Cod made a perfect pair in my book.

"Let's check in with Randi," Jamie said to me.

"Right! The fun should start soon," I answered.

We sneaked around the dark gym and crept into our prearranged meeting place—a shadowy gap between the bleachers along the wall. Randi was there waiting for us. Since we were close to the refreshment stand, we could watch Mandy and keep out of sight at the same time.

"They just left the punch bowl," Randi said as she pointed out Chris and Mandy. Chris had just handed Mandy a glass of punch. "This should be good," Randi continued. "I fixed it so every boy in the place is expecting to dance with Mandy . . . including Todd Jackson."

Jamie and I snickered.

"Quiet! Look," Jamie instructed. Before Mandy could drink her punch, a boy with black hair came up to her holding two cups of punch.

"Here's the drink you asked me to get, Mandy," the boy said.

"What?" Mandy asked as Chris smiled and backed away from her.

"I said . . . here's your punch," the boy repeated as he shoved the cup at her. Mandy looked around for Chris to help. But he just shrugged. She didn't know what to do. So she took the cup.

Then two more boys came up holding cups of punch.

"Here's your drink, Mandy," said one.

"I found you at last," said the other. "Are you still thirsty?"

They shoved cups of punch at Mandy. She could hardly hold them all. "What is going on?" Mandy said in a puzzled tone. She really was baffled.

Another boy came up with punch. He saw all the cups. "Wow, you must drink like a camel," the boy said.

The band started to play. "My dance," one of the boys said. Chris glanced over at us, winking.

"She promised it to me," said another.

"You're wrong," shouted yet another guy. "This is my dance."

The boys surrounded Mandy. They pulled her back and forth as they argued over who would get to dance with her.

"Wait! Stop! Hold it!" ordered Mandy. "I didn't agree to dance with any of you."

"Yes, you did!" they said. And they pointed out the places in the gym where they'd met up with Mandy.

"That's impossible," Mandy tried to explain. "I've been right here by the refreshment stand the whole time," she insisted. "And one person can't be in two or more places at once." Mandy kept talking and explaining, but the boys refused to listen.

"Well, who are you going to dance with?" one of the boys wanted to know.

"She's going to dance with me," someone grunted. The circle of guys around Mandy parted. There stood Todd the Cod Jackson. "This is my dance!" he announced.

Mandy took one look at Todd and gulped. "You have to get Chris's permission first," she said. And she looked at Chris in a pleading fashion. She wanted him to say no.

"It's fine with me," Chris replied.

But luck was with Mandy at that minute. Just then the music stopped.

"Sorry, the dance is over," Mandy said.

But before Mandy could protest further, the band started a slow dance. The Cod took her hand and led her out onto the floor. No one dared protest, not even Mandy.

Awkwardly, they stumbled around the floor, bumping into people left and right. Every other step Todd took squashed one of Mandy's toes. It really was hilarious!

Chris took the opportunity to join us. "I'd almost feel sorry for Mandy if I could stop laughing," Chris said.

"Now she knows what it's like to have someone imitate her," I said.

"She's getting just what she deserves," Randi added.

The music stopped. But Todd the Cod refused to turn Mandy loose. She ended up getting stuck with him for two more dances. By the time they finished dancing, I don't think she had a toe that wasn't smashed.

When the band finally stopped playing to take a short break, Mandy made a quick exit. She rushed off, leaving the Cod standing there alone as she headed for the refreshments. But this time there was only one person waiting for her with a cup of punch. It was Bobbi Joy Boikin!

"Uh-oh!" Jamie said when she saw Bobbi Joy. "Look!"

"Should we go to her rescue?" asked Chris as he glanced first at Randi and then at me.

"Maybe we'd better," I suggested. "Bobbi Joy looks really mad."

Randi nodded. "Let's go!" We dashed across the floor.

"I warned you to stay away from him," Bobbi Joy said to Mandy in a nasty way.

"What are you talking about?" answered Mandy, totally puzzled.

"Leave her alone, Bobbi," I ordered as we walked up.

"Watch out! She knows karate, Bobbi Joy," warned Randi.

For the first time, Mandy realized we were at the dance. She got a good look at our clothes and our hair. "Wait a second," she said. "What's going on. . . . Hey, I get it. . . ." She laughed and nodded in understanding. "Now everything makes sense. You found out that I pretended to be you, so you two pretended to be me. I guess acting runs in our family, huh?"

"Naturally," I replied. "We're a gifted family."

"This makes us even," Randi said to Mandy.

"And you were all in on it," Mandy said to Chris and Jamie. They both grinned and nodded.

"What is all this baloney?" Bobbi Joy grunted.

"It was all a joke, Bobbi," I explained.

"Oh, yeah! Well the joke's on her!" Bobbi snapped. She dipped her fingers into her cup of punch and flicked the droplets at Mandy. They splattered on Mandy's face and dripped all over her special sweater. If Mandy really knew karate, that was sure the time to use it. But she didn't do anything. She just stood there gasping and dripping red punch.

"That was a crummy thing to do," Randi said to Bobbi Joy. Bobbi Joy just laughed in Randi's face. Then she dipped her fingers in the cup again and flicked punch at Randi.

"How dare you do that to my cousin!" roared Mandy angrily. "*Hieeyah!*" she screamed and leaped into a karate fight stance.

Bobbi Joy was caught completely off guard. She was so shocked she staggered backward and bumped into the refreshment table, knocking it over. The table fell to the floor and the plastic punch bowl went flying. Bobbi fell to the floor and the contents of the punch bowl spilled all over Bobbi. She ended up getting a tropical punch shower. The entire gym burst into laughter. It seemed that Bobbi Joy's bullying days were over for good. After all, a person can't be a bully and the laughingstock of the school both at the same time!

"You were terrific!" Randi said.

Miss Morgan and Coach Matthews came running up. "What happened?" the coach asked as he looked at Bobbi Joy sitting in a pool of punch.

"Bobbi Joy accidentally spilled the punch," I explained.

Coach Matthews helped Bobbi Joy to her feet. "You'd better go home and change," he told her. "Don't worry about the mess. I'll have it cleaned up."

Bobbi Joy nodded and staggered off with

Todd the Cod helping her. They left the gym and that was the last we saw of them that night.

Miss Morgan looked at Mandy's sweater. "That's going to leave an awful stain," Miss Morgan said as she handed Mandy some napkins. "How did it happen?"

"I was a little clumsy," Mandy said as she wiped her face. "I spilled my drink."

"I guess you won't want to go onstage and sing for us now," Miss Morgan continued.

"Sing? I volunteered to sing in front of everyone?" Mandy sputtered.

"Yes, don't you remember?" Miss Morgan asked.

Mandy looked at me. She glanced at Randi. We smiled and nodded. "Oh, I remember now," Mandy replied. The three of us burst out laughing.

"You mean you'll still go on?" Miss Morgan asked.

"Sure. Why not?" Mandy said. "The show

must go on even if I'm not a very good singer." She winked at us.

"You're a good sport," Miss Morgan told Mandy.

"And I think you're a pretty good cousin, too," I added. "Now that I finally got to know the real you."

"I agree," Randi said.

"Do you want to dance?" Chris asked Jamie.

"Sure," replied Jamie as they walked toward the middle of the gym.

Mandy smiled at us. "I think from now on I'm going to be the real me all the time."

"And I'm going to be the real me," Randi kidded. "Every time I pretend to be Sandi or you, I end up in trouble."

"I think this is going to be a great summer after all," I said. Mandy and Randi agreed.

"It'll be great once I get this singing thing over with," Mandy corrected. "I really do have a rotten voice."

"Well, let's be rotten together," I suggested.

"You mean . . . all sing?" Randi gulped.

"That's right," I said. "In the Daniels family, we stick together!"

"Hey! I knew it would be great to be part of a big family," Mandy admitted. "Especially when you're about to make a fool of yourself!"

*   *   *   *   *

On the way home from the dance, all we could talk about was our singing debut.

"You were a smash," Chris said as he walked alongside us.

"What hams," Jamie added.

"Admit it! We were good," Randi said.

"Sandi was good," Mandy corrected. "We just followed her lead."

"All three of us were good," I said as we stopped at the corner where Jamie and Chris had to turn off

"Bye! See you tomorrow," we called as they walked away.

The rest of the way home we sang at the top of our lungs. We didn't stop singing until we opened the door of the house and stepped in.

"Where is everybody?" Randi called.

"We're in the kitchen having ice cream," Dad answered.

"Chock-a-lott ice tream," Teddy said as we entered. "It's dood!" he yelled, jerking his arms upward. As he did, the ice cream on his spoon went flying into the air.

SPLAT! A big glob of gooey ice cream landed right on Mandy's head.

"First my favorite sweater gets ruined," Mandy groaned. "Now there's ice cream in my hair," she griped. "There's only one thing to do with a kid like you, Teddy," she grumbled as she moved closer to him with her arms outstretched. "Do you know what that is?"

"What?" Teddy gulped.

"Kiss him!" Mandy laughed as she bent over and plastered a big wet kiss on Teddy's chubby cheek.

Fifteen

THE rest of the summer seemed to fly by. Before I knew it, we were back at the airport waiting for Mandy to board her plane for home. Great times always seem to pass too fast.

"Now don't forget," Mandy said to Randi and me. "Next summer you're both coming to Hollywood to visit with me."

We nodded. Mom and Dad had already promised we could go.

"We're going to miss you," Mom said as she hugged and kissed Mandy.

"We sure are," I added. Sentimental me. I was the first one to cry. Then everybody started blubbering.

"Good-bye, Trouble," Mandy said as she picked up Teddy and gave him a big bear hug.

"Bye, Manee," he said after she put him down.

"Now stay right here, Teddy," I instructed as I sniffed. We all started to wave as Mandy walked off to board her plane.

"Bye, everyone! I had a great time. Bye!" And then Mandy was gone.

"Let's go up to the observation deck and watch her plane take off," Dad suggested.

"Great idea," Randi agreed. She turned to take Teddy's hand. He wasn't where I had told him to stand. "Oh, no, not again!" Randi yelled. "Hey, Teddy's gone!"

We all did a double-take and frantically looked around.

"TEDDY! TEDDY!" we called.

"I right here," Teddy answered. He was at a nearby trash can throwing away the paper to the candy bar he'd unwrapped.

"I thought I told you to stand right here!" I scolded. I was as angry as I was relieved. "From now on, do what I tell you."

Teddy slowly shook his head. "Sanee not da boss," Trouble said as he bit into his candy bar. "Ranee not da boss. Manee not da boss. I da boss!"

And we didn't want to, but we all laughed. We couldn't help it. The way he said it was just so funny!

About the Author

MICHAEL J. PELLOWSKI was born in New Brunswick, New Jersey. He is a graduate of Rutgers the State University of New Jersey, and has a degree in education. Before turning to writing he was a professional football player and then a high school teacher.

He is married to Judith Snyder Pellowski, his former high school sweetheart. They have four children, Morgan, Matthew, Melanie, and Martin. They have one cat, Kitty, and two cocker spaniels, Spike and Brandie.

Michael has written more than 125 books for children. He is currently writing scripts for a popular comic book series. When he's not writing books, Michael enjoys fishing with his family as well as jogging and exercising.